DISTINCTION

and Other Stories

A Collection of Short Stories by George Horsman

Published by New Generation Publishing in 2018

First Edition

www.newgeneration-publishing.com

CONTENTS

Distinction

'They've got beef for lunch. Probably black market but we don't need to know about that.

'It's not what we eat. It's what we're going to talk about.'

'Don't worry. Daddy'll settle that.' 'You make him sound like a dictator.'

'He is rather. But lovely, when you know him.'

The Principal's reputation wasn't lovely.

Archibald Alexander Peebles ruled the ancient pile by commandments issued as if from Mount Sinai. The man who'd bludgeoned Senate into waiving fees for the children of professors and Principals. Who'd insisted on a special allowance for distinguished scholars. Rick swallowed. Life in the Ulster Rifles was child's play compared with this.

'Have you really never seen him?'

'No, I'd no idea he was your… And he was away on his goodwill trip to Bermuda when we had the freshers' introductory talk.'

'He doesn't give that anyway. He doesn't approve of students.' 'Not even ex-service?'

'Mm.' Angela wriggled an enchanting nose. 'Maybe. He was in the Army, you know.

He was an adjutant.'

A faint bell in Rick's brain drowned under the rattle of Angela's key in the mansion's front door. As it opened there issued forth an aroma of black-market beef basted in what must surely have been above-rations butter. No need to know about that. Adjusting the level of his gaze, he studied the small woman who appeared in the hall.

'Ah.' The accent was Sloane Square. No, Glasgow Kelvinside. She held out a hand, palm down, in a way which sparked a momentary impulse to kneel and kiss it. 'You must be Richard.'

‘Rick – well, I mean, yes, Richard. I suppose. How do you do?’

He wasn’t doing very well. Angela puffed her cheeks and chest in reproof. The promontories bounced enthrallingly. He couldn’t wait to get her back to Dame Agnes Kilcraggan Hall. Before male visitors’ chucking-out time - six o’clock. Even before that, the rules obliged them to push the bed out of the door. Thank heavens for a soft hearthrug.

Mrs Peebles led them into the dining room. The ceiling supported a chandelier over a long table laden with dishes of vegetables and a huge hemispherical silver dome presumably covering the beef of unknown origin. At the other end a man sat staring into space: Archibald Alexander.

He didn’t get up, merely nodded to them to sit down. Rick concealed a glance at his five-shilling watch. Unless the hairspring had gone haywire again, it was two minutes past one. Late again, Second Lieutenant Belper. They sat with lowered eyes while the Principal said grace.

‘…and sae the Laird be thankit.’

Curious that a man who’d ironed from his speech every trace of a Govan upbringing in favour of a Paramount News bray should choose a Scottish grace. To prove his authenticity? That would be it. Rick let his host begin to eat, then picked up the corresponding cutlery. For some minutes Mrs Peebles talked with cold earnestness about social acquaintances – all, it seemed, Honourables or with double-barrelled names. It was the build-up to thunder. They waited tensely.

‘So I understand you wish my daughter’s hand in marriage?’

Rick fought down a hiccup. It wasn’t her *hand* so much. *No!* He checked himself. *For Heaven’s sake don’t say that. And don’t get pushed into asking his permission.*

On the other hand, they’d need wedding presents, money. Best play safe. ‘Er well yes, we’re engaged and plan to marry soon.’

'Urrhum. A most momentous step in a man's life.'

But what if the man's wife obeyed his every whim? Didn't that make it easier? Rick's eyes strayed to their hostess. Nesta Peebles was known among the University's undergraduates as Nessie, but the monster of Loch Ness didn't fit that face with its sweat of insecure social aspiration. He performed a mime of agreement.

It was a relief when Peebles shifted to the topic he found most absorbing. 'I myself have found the married state most satisfactory. So far.'

Oh, a turn up for the books, eh? Good for you? Been all right, has she? But every reply was inappropriate. Fortunately, none seemed called for. Rick raised his eyebrows in feigned delight.

'I married as soon as my dissertation was accepted and I was awarded the accolade of a permanent appointment.'

Rick gave his royal-command performance an encore. Stick with a winning game.

'Marriage played a part, small but important, in assisting me throughout a career of unprecedented success in the University - my anthology of poetry from nineteenth- century

Asuncion; my many well-regarded articles in the quality press; my translation of Paraguay's national epic poem, *The Lands to West* .'

Ah, *The Lands to West.* Rick had heard of that. He'd seen a canto in translation reprinted in the *Saturday Evening Post* – the part where a Paraguayan force invading Bolivia reaches a remote village and the soldiers have it off with local girls. No doubt as to why the *Post* wanted to reprint that. Sheer love of poetry. Jolly good job literary sex didn't conflict with Archibald Alexander's well-known thunderings against pornography. How disastrous if literature and life started mixing.

'All this was interrupted by military service of some distinction during the war.'

Rick accepted Mrs Peebles' silent offer of salt. 'You were clearly in the thick of things. Let me guess: Alamein?

Salerno? Normandy?'

Peebles' abstracted smile showed no awareness of the question. Weren't there philosophers who believed that only they existed?

'I was regimental adjutant in the Ulster Rifles. I served on the Continent after D-Day.'

'My! You saw heavy fighting, then?'

'I remained in County Down throughout the actual hostilities, being posted out only in June 1945.'

Rick reached again for his wine. From first sight of Peebles, unease had troubled him. There was something about the voice, the name. And '*Ulster Rifles*'! Memory stirred. The past slipped into the room like an agent in some spy film, sinister and ominous.

It had been the Medical Officer whom Rick had gone to see. With VE Day over, the Battalion had moved to Brussels, setting up HQ in a once magnificent but now run-down hotel while they recuperated after a mauling at the hands of Model's retreating army. But it wasn't German shells that had worried Rick most. While his ears still cracked with the blast of explosions and the air rattled with remembered gunfire what enveloped him was the heavy- hanging, sore bloat in the groin, the unstaunchable suppurations. How narrowly a man's real concerns focussed.

'*Tu veux passer du bon temps?*' the girl in Liege had asked.

He'd followed her into the doorway. A likeable kid – *sympathique,* despite her soulless job. The friendliness made her later legacy seem somehow worse: a postponed betrayal. His gaze had wandered with nervy unsteadiness round the battalion's improvised surgery as he acquainted the M.O. with his problem.

'Take a few weeks off till you pull round.' The duty captain handed him the expected antibiotics. 'And no more exercise of that kind. It'll mean you miss parades. Better explain to the adjutant.' He jerked a thumb towards the office one floor up. 'He's in now.'

And there, enthroned at a desk immaculately devoid of papers, had sat Archibald Alexander.

'After my third tour of duty in Latin America I made the time to lead a fact-finding mission to Africa, a continent hitherto beyond the scope of my expertise…'

But with a giant intellect like yours…

'With me, however, to remedy that was but the work of a few days …'

Of course. Yet a dreadful uncertainty lingered. Did the Great Sage recognise, in the claimant for his daughter's hand, the seedy youth with bug-infested genitals who'd laid his dose before him in the *Hotel de la Paix* eighteen months earlier? Rick crouched over the mystically-engendered beef. If only his own origins could remain as obscure.

The Principal expatiated on his achievements in Latin American scholarship, the honours he'd received, his contempt for the peasants and illiterate labourers of the region. How could Angela be this man's daughter? Someone so fresh and genuine. Was it *possible*?

Eventually Peebles paused and Nessie took up the conversation. Her upper-crust credentials now established, she turned to social issues.

'All this talk of wartime illegitimacies and extra-marital…' Her voice tailed away at the unspeakable word. She waved a gracious hand in concession to the unnamed talkers' misguidedness. 'It's just the lowest classes. No one else behaves like that.' The disgust seemed to apply to all relationships, even marital. How had Angela ever come into the world?

Even departure an hour later, the visit over, brought little relief. There'd been no perceptible recognition, no outburst as Peebles remembered the hangdog subaltern that frosty Brussels morning. Yet surely memory had stirred some ripple in the still pool of solipsism?

At the front porch Rick closed the door with unintended vigour.

'Shsh.' Angela reproved him. 'Not so strong. You see,

it was nice. He's lovely, isn't he?'

Rick assumed a smile, regal and beatific, gazing at the girl he knew better than anyone in the world, and not at all.

Taken At The Flood

Even after forty years away, Ethel's skin crept with fear.

Sight of what had been Shotfield's main street, the brook that had run along one side of it now dried up, the roadway pooled and pitted from the weight of water it had borne for so long, brought back memories of the man's sinister presence. Grindley, the village idiot, had been far more malign than his usual nickname allowed. She remembered the times he'd lain in wait for her on her weekly walk to the grocery store. The day he'd hustled her into Church Alley and laid oil-stained fingers on her dress. Worse still, there'd been those months when, desperate for employment, she'd taken a job as his assistant at the cold store behind Metcalf's Garage. In many ways it had been a relief when Manchester Water broke its dramatic news. The village was to be raised, drowned under twenty billion gallons of a new reservoir's water. Everyone in Shotfield would have to move.

With care she negotiated the pools still cratering the footpath. Even the summer's drought with its water rationing hadn't dried them up entirely. But almost everything else stood cleansed in air and sunshine. Miss Blyth's post office had been here. Across the road Len Carter's smithy had released a sour singe as horses' hooves were branded for shoeing. All that remained now were the bases of rough chalk walls, an architect's plan of the drowned village. She'd never thought to see the place again. Only reports in the papers had brought her back despite the quaking of legs and stomach, hurrying to beat the downpours that were now ending the country's drought further north.

At the village's end she halted. The square of land at the roadside was unrecognisable now, the canopy demolished, petrol pumps removed. But there could be no doubt. This was Metcalf's Garage. And round the back…

For a moment her bowels melted. But reason steadied them. It was forty years ago.

Single and without living relations, she'd left no address when she moved. For half a lifetime she'd been swallowed up in London, without link or contact with Shotfield. Grindley couldn't get her now. She turned towards the cold store.

What made fear linger, she realised, was that he still had a motive: revenge. That last day, the day of the final evacuation after loudspeaker cars had patrolled the streets telling stragglers to leave, making sure no one remained, she'd slipped back to the cold store for a fleece jacket she'd left behind. And there, inside the freeze room, Grindley had been waiting. 'Lost something?'

'Nothing.' She knew with exact terror what he wanted her to lose.

'Where are you off to?'

'I want my fleece. There it is.'

She moved forward to take it from a slatted wooden shelf but he was too quick. He dangled it high in the air, taunting.

'Where are you going when you leave Shotfield?'

'What's that to you? Please give it me.'

She made a grab but in vain. He moved forward, his stained teeth grinning, his halitosis faecal. She shrank back against the open steel door the demolition men had left intact, an offering to the slow levellers of rust and grime.

What happened next she couldn't bring herself to dwell on. The frantic struggle, the pincers of his fingers on her arm, her cry as a hand invaded her clothing, then – her last resort – the sinking of teeth into his wrist, the soggy give of skin breaking, salt blood, then unstable feet carrying her out of the store as fast as panic could move them. The door slamming shut behind her, the fleece abandoned, her only purpose to reach the bus stop with its human shield of others awaiting departure, Mrs Mitton minding her luggage.

Unsteady with recollection, she crossed the garage

forecourt. He couldn't possibly be there. The fear was mad. How could it, over all these years, have coated her mind so constantly with its sickness? He must be seventy now or – but a young girl has no idea of adults' ages.

The brick-built office and passageway had been flattened in the flood. But steel was durable. Intent on following the foundations of the walls, she almost collided with the freeze room.

No longer smart in cream paint but flecked and pitted in a hundred places as if by shrapnel fragments, it stood on its levelled site like the hull of some sunken ship. One side of its roof had crumpled under the weight of water, giving it the slew of a car with a puncture. Ethel could imagine fish darting through its pockmarks, nosing along the dints and creases in its side.

She raised a hand to the door. The handle had always been heavy. She remembered struggling with it on her first day at work, shoving and wrestling, desperate not to ask Grindley for help. Now it hung black and clotted, a diseased member, sealing the cabin that, in her life's one act of violence, had seen both her and her tormentor wounded - he for a month, she for life. His presence was there now.

You're mad, Ethel. He's old, or dead. That's why you've come. To wipe out the past, the fear of men it's left you with, the loneliness that has come with it. This is so you can start living.

She pressed down the handle. Sludged with water-weed, it resisted her palm painfully. She pressed harder, then harder still. At last, with a wrenching sound like a childhood tooth coming out – why did all the images centre on childhood – the black steel tongue snapped, coming apart in her hand, a knife caked with black blood. She thought, now I can't get in.

But the force of gravity told otherwise. With a small lurch, the door opened a crack, then swung wider and, as when a theatre's curtains part, she found herself staring into black space, the scene of that last bitter quarrel.

It all came back. The dreadful fight, her staggering away, the click of the door closing at her back. The ineradicable image of his black teeth, grinning.

In that moment the tic returned. It had visited her through her teens and twenties in bed at night at Mrs Proctor's in Battersea: the to-and-fro flickering of her head as if from stinging insects; the fusing of organs in her stomach. In her early thirties it had dwindled and with its departure she'd started to hope the past could be erased. But liberation never came. Memories of Shotfield stalked her every day. It's over she'd told herself. You mustn't let it ruin the present, the future. *Why can't I forget?*

It was on her thirty-fifth birthday that she realised she never would. The young Canadian had been so polite and kind, a tall handsome man, asking her out to dinner, choosing a lovely restaurant. But, as so often before, appetite deserted her. Without saliva, too nerve-racked even to swallow, she'd pushed the expensive food aside untouched. Even the attempt to speak left her whispering, a blotchy microphone struggling to utter sound. The mere memory of the disgrace was unbearable.

She stepped into the freeze room. Silence, but for one faint click. As her eyes adjusted, she saw that the room wasn't quite black. Tiny patches of the roof had caved away, letting pencils of sunlight prod down. How ordinary it looked, not at all like the submerged *Titanic* she'd imagined. She made out a murky box, some shelves darkened as if still wet, the light bulb's filament amazingly intact under broken glass. Was this the banal scene that had bedevilled her for a lifetime?

Something lay on the floor among some old boxes. *Melville. Pendle Street, Carlisle.* She could still read a fruit wholesaler's stencilled name on one of them. She kicked it aside, then another. Then withdrew her foot. On the toecap something glutinous was sticking. She bent and peered at it through the half-light. Sweat broke cold on her back and forehead. She looked again behind the boxes.

And caught breath.

A man, recognisable not from the purulent face or weed-slithery hands but by his boiler suit and yellow boots, lay there, bloated and greasy. Grindley.

Horror trembled through her. Sickness. Then, as she recaptured breath, bewilderment.

Why was he here? How had it happened? And with the cabin's door openable from inside? But slowly memory seeped back. Manufactured in the early post-war years, the room had, like most refrigerators of the day, been an austerity product. The sneck-lock, difficult to manage from outside, had been worse inside. Fleeing in terror, she'd slammed the door. Grindley had tried to follow. She remembered the click as it swung shut. But the lock must have jammed. With no one nearby to hear his shouts, and the store soundproof, he'd been left without food, drink or any renewal of air as the reservoir's water slowly rose round the steel sarcophagus. And over him.

Giddy, she slumped down on to a box. She had killed him. In a scald of guilt she shut her eyes, desperate to clamp out the past. But there was no hope; never had been. As the neural tic jolted again and again the fact took root that her fear of Grindley's reappearance over all those years had been utterly groundless. For him there'd been no way out. And now only her guilt was inescapable.

As inescapable as the small stream now entering the cabin through cracks in the floor, growing deeper, as the brook running through the village refilled from the storms to the north, reclaiming its lost empire, refilling every cavity with deep, resistless water.

Oh, How We Danced

Move me into the sun.. Well, not the sun exactly. More probably the operating theatre in half an hour's time if they're working to schedule, which they won't be. It's Wilfred Owen, isn't it, the bit about the sun? To do with a soldier's death. And now my turn.

Because there will be a death; oh yes, there'll be a death. One they don't reckon with, these doctors and nurses. 'Have you ever suffered from any of the following?' Mr Bellis the surgeon asked, checking that I was fit to go under the knife. But I didn't tell him. Not about my allergy to anaesthetics and the terrifying form it takes. Not about the time they switched on the ether after my climbing accident and the reaction was so extreme it would have killed me if Ljubo hadn't intervened and made them stop the operation. Why bother resurrecting that? Why should I cling to life, an old woman like me with a thousand yesterdays and no tomorrow? The rodent's already gnawing inside me, in several places. All they'd do would be to delay the inevitable.

And so I lie here, waiting for my grandson, Wayne, to call - waiting for the call in more than one sense, you could say - and, while I wait, listening to old-time tunes played on someone's radio in the next ward. What passing bells are these? Wrong again, Wilfred. Not passing bells. It's Joe Loss or Edmundo Ros or whatever wizard it was that conducted the Palm Court Orchestra back in the 'forties. That thrilling slur of the strings, the heart-stopping swoop of the clarinets. How it brings time back! I could measure out my life in yesteryear's tunes.

Oh how we danced on the night we were wed! Hear it? There's a song I shall never separate from moving memories: the all-enveloping white dress, Ernest's dignity and aristocratic bearing as we walked down the aisle at St Margaret's, Westminster, the tumult of the organ, the groaning tables afterwards at The George in Southwark and the waltzes and foxtrots far into the night, until a limousine came and spirited us away to our week in post-war Bournemouth. What style we showed! What evening-dress formality and propriety! By the time we arrived, Ernest and I were too exhausted to make love but it didn't matter, seeing we'd been doing it, shockingly in those days, for months?

It was all a dream, of course, a bubble. And like any other bubble, it burst.

People think that's tragic, the death of romance. But for me the important thing is to have had romance, to have felt it at least once, not that it should last for ever. Why should it? Nothing does. It's asking too much of life. And the point is, something else comes along, some other person or passion, and your momentum comes back. You've simply changed your source of power.

With me the momentum came partly from work: it was about then that I was made Head of my section in the Ministry, the youngest there'd ever been. And partly it was Ljubo. He was so handsome. Six foot tall and broad-built, he had that high- cheeked Slavic face that seemed to have a faint touch of the orient about it. And despite everything the prosecution said in court, he was a man of integrity. He believed in his system of government and I believed in ours.

Of course I made a fool of myself, telling him what I did across the pillow, but how could I not? When you're in love you can't hide things. You tell all you know; it's a form of giving. If I'd thought of the Official Secrets Act as we nestled between the sheets it wouldn't have been love. And it wouldn't have been me.

Listen. Can you hear it? *We are in love with you, my heart and I.* Always one of my favourites.

It wasn't until the trial was over and I was languishing in jail underneath Lancaster Castle, the same jail that had once housed Roundheads and Jacobites, witches and supporters of hunchback Richard (not such bad company when you think of today's politicians), that I realised what a blessing Ljubo had unintendedly been.

You see, in court I’d proved that Christine wasn't Ljubo's daughter - she was born before our romance began - and so by some slip of logic everyone assumed she must be Ernest's. And that's what they’ve gone on believing ever since.

It isn't true, of course. I've never told anyone, just let sleeping dogs lie. But Ernest's not in this world any more now and Ljubo's long since gone back to whatever they call his part of Yugoslavia nowadays; so why not? The remnant of my days is shortening, like the beams from a car's headlights when you come to rising ground. Or like walking the plank. Why not speak before you reach the end, the sudden, breath- catching fall, the rush of the brine of mortality into the lungs? So I will. It took time to work out the dates but once I did there was no doubt. Christine was born not to

Ernest but to another lover, Alan - someone I used to see while Ernest was away on his frequent forays to slaughter defenceless grouse and deer.

Not even Christine knows that. And I shan't tell her. She's had troubles enough.

Let her go on believing she bears a likeness to Ernest, feeling proud of the stolidity and sense she thinks she's inherited.

After a year they let me out of jail on day-release. A new university was being built a few miles away and I went to work in the library: a special arrangement made through the good offices of an old friend in the government, Wesley Craig - Sir Wesley - who I'd known since childhood. As children we played together on our families’ adjacent estates in Argyll. Wesley always said the library job was his repayment for my letting him win at croquet: I always did. So, a piece of luck.

But then another followed. Luck evens out, you know, provided you take enough risks to let it. At any rate, one afternoon as I was leaving the library who should turn up, admitted as a special reader for the day, but one of my old executive officers at the Ministry, Jonathan James. Almost blind, soon to become totally so. He always says he was sent to do some research for a Ministry publication he was preparing; but I think he hooked the job so he could see me. At any rate within three months we were married and I could change my infamous name to his: Mrs James. Our joke was that he was James the First, I was James the Second and my temporary successor at the Ministry, a phoney if ever there was one, was the Old Pretender.

Poor blind old bat, how I love him. Even now I'm hospitalised and he's in a nursing home, the fire still burns. For all those years of our marriage I had to fill in his tax return, and keep him up to date with what was happening on the news, while until retirement I was passing my days in a purposeless bureaucratic job, again wangled through family contacts. But I never wished it to be otherwise. He was my support far more than I was his. And still is. He's what's left of my career and my life. He's all I want.

Hear it? *Falling in love with love is falling for make-believe*. Yes, I remember that one. It unrolls the years. I'm glad to be past that.

Hello, do I hear the patter of..? But my! Was I going to say ‘tiny feet’? Not so tiny now. Soon big enough to go to school.

Wayne, come in! I can't imagine in what wild-west moment Christine gave you that name but anyway it's wonderful to see you. Give me a hug! Lovely! And you've brought flowers! My, how beautiful! Put them in that water-jug someone brought me as a belated wedding present. As if I'd drink water!

And your Mum's let you get the bus across town on your own, because she's too busy with her television work to come herself. Well, I suppose we all have to put first things first. If we know which they are. It’s just like Christine, that. Like so many of her generation. Like her brother, Lionel, and his wife. They’re tough as old nails, Wayne. What, another hug? Doesn't your mum ever hug you? Never mind, dear.

Granny loves you. While she's around.

Wayne, since you're here and since, well, we might not get another chance to speak in private, can I tell you something? Yes, a secret. As if we're a gang and have taken an oath signed in blood. You've done that sometimes, with your pals, haven't you? Good. Then you'll know what I mean.

The secret's this, Wayne. I've left you all my money. When I go, I mean. People come to visit me here, distant relations who hear I'm old and not too well, and what they're really hoping is that their names will appear in my will, alongside Lionel's and Christine's. But those relations won't be there and neither will Lionel or Christine. It's not that I don't love them but they're dripping money as it is, and so are most of Christine's and Lionel's lovers. I've never heard of one who didn't sound at least at Bond Street level.

So I've left everything to you. Not to Ellis or Timothy, though they're my grandchildren, too, Lionel's children. No, just to you. And there's a reason. I'm going to tell you it, Wayne, because I want you to know how special you are. Not only to everyone who meets you but especially to me. It's the reason I let your mother send you along by yourself today, the reason why I even encouraged her a little to devote the afternoon to her television work. It was what she wanted anyway.

And this is my reason. You mustn't be upset by it. It doesn't mean you're any less loved. You see, because of the way Lionel and his wife have led their lives with their open marriage - and who would I be to blame them for that - I can't be sure, perhaps *they* can't be sure, whose children Ellis and Timothy really are. Whereas at least we know you're Christine's, and therefore my grandson. You're the only one I know for sure is my blood and bones, whoever contributed the rest. That's why I've left everything to you. Selfish, isn't it? But an old woman's allowed a few vices.

Here they come now with that trolley-bed-thing.

They're coming to get me, for the operation. Give me a kiss, Wayne. There. You'll always remember our little talk today, won't you? Always. Even if we never have another. Yes, nurse, I'm coming.

Be happy, Wayne, with all your wealth and your memories. The others won't like what I've done but don't be upset, only be generous. Think of it as a special favour that all I have is going to you.

Well, not quite all. There is another legacy, a small one, just ten thousand pounds. A bequest like that will mean a lot to Ljubo.

Don't watch me being wheeled out. Just listen.

Oh the song of the Kerry dancing, Oh, the ring of the piper's tune.
Oh, for one of those hours of gladness,
Gone, alas, like our youth, too soon.

Just Good Friends

'You married, then?'

The girl jerked her head up and down, staring ahead through the windscreen. 'Your old man, then, doesn't he mind - you on the game like this?'

'Nah.'

'Perhaps he don't know? Keep it secret like?' 'He doesn't say nothing.'

'But he guesses? Two nights a week you say you're out. He must wonder.' 'I say I'm at bingo. Like, in a way, I am. Game of chance.'

Ron uttered a short laugh and, overcoming reluctance, the girl joined in.

She eyed her wristwatch. 'Time we was moving.' 'Yeh, yeh. I'm only interested. Nice girl like you.'

He opened his mouth to go on, but a tap on the car window cut him short. Turning, he glimpsed a dark uniform, a peak cap. His movements slowed. 'Oh Gawd, not them.' Toilsomely he unwound the window.

'Good evening, sir. Sorry to trouble you but I happened to see you stopping your car and accosting this young lady here, just by the CCTV camera. As you know, kerb - crawling's an offence under the law and I'm obliged to book anyone found doing it.'

Ron raised a distressed hand to his face. The back of it was black with hairs – far more numerous than those left on his prematurely balding head.

'No, officer, you're making a mistake. This lady's a friend of mine. Known each other a long time, we have. I was just offering her a lift home.'

The constable tapped a pencil against his notepad. 'Well, that's interesting. Is it far, then, back to where the young lady lives?'

'Oh, well now.' The redundant words provided time for thought. 'Yes, quite a way, really. Far enough for her to need help getting back.'

'It'll be near your own house, I expect, with you being old friends?' 'Well, yes, you could say that. Not far apart at all.'

'You see quite a bit of each other, do you? Dropping in to each other's houses, like, being close neighbours?'

'Yeh. Has been known.'

The constable flexed his notepad. 'Anyway, I'd be grateful if you'd be so good as to give me your name and address – just for the record.'

'Well, yes.' The driver fidgeted in his seat in a manner suggesting ant-bites. 'So…?'

'Oh yes. I'm Arthur Symington. 148 Wellesley Road. I can write it down for you.' 'No, thank you very much. Wellesley Road. Number one -four-eight. That it? Er, could I just see your driving licence, please, to check the spelling?'

'Spelling's fine.' 'Just to check.'

The man calling himself Arthur Symington clapped hands to his pockets, punctuating his search with a barrage of exclamations. 'Well, blow me. Sorry, officer, I don't seem to have it with me. Not like me at all, that isn't.'

'Well, at least you'll be able to give me the young lady's name. Being close friends and neighbours, as you are.'

'Wouldn't it be better if she herself –? '

He turned to his companion but as the girl's lips opened, red and ripe as camellia blossoms, the policeman's hand rose in veto. For a moment it wavered as if uncertain of purpose, but then, descending towards her person, almost settled on a naked shoulder before its owner checked himself. 'If you don't mind, I'd prefer it if you was to tell me. What's the young lady's name, then?'

'Well, darn me. That's one of the things about working all hours, you don't remember names so well, not like you once did. I'm really angry 'bout that, I really am. Head like a sieve.'

'You're saying you've forgotten?'

‘I’d never have believed it if you’d have told me.’

‘And her address. Where you go when you just drop in on her, like you and your family often do?’

‘Nah. You don’t remember numbers, do you? Once you’ve been there and know the way there’s no need for street names.’

But the constable had stepped aside, taking notes as he scanned the car’s number plate. In a moment he returned. ‘There’s an easy solution for getting the young lady’s address.’ He took from his breast pocket a mobile phone. He held it out. ‘How about if you was to ring your wife? She’d be sure to know, wouldn’t she?’

The driver’s distress was intense now. As he broke into protest, stressing his wife’s poor memory and cursing his own forgetfulness in all matters involving numbers, globules of saliva from a reddened face spattered down on the girl’s black leather miniskirt and the varnish of tights encased beneath it. Only after several minutes did the splutter at last die. The constable was first to break silence.

‘I think it would be better if you were to tell the truth, sir. It’s be simpler and the consequences of a guilty plea would be less severe.’

The man called Arthur Symington swallowed but the action misfired and for a minute he was enveloped in a fit of coughing. ‘All right, officer,’ he said at last. ‘What’s the damage? What’s the on-the-spot fine for it?’

‘I’m afraid it’s not an on-the-spot sort of offence, sir. It’ll need to go to the magistrates.’

‘Oh Gawd. But I can pay. I’ve got the ready.’

‘Sorry, sir. The lady can go. It’d be hard to prove anything against her, seeing you did the accosting, and in any case’ – he peered at the girl’s pale face – ‘Sasha, isn’t it? We are acquainted It’s not long since Sasha made her latest appearance at Earl Street. We can give her a rest tonight. So to speak.’

But another idea dawned on Symington’s face. From an inside pocket he drew a wallet and brandished it, though without clear meaning. ‘So I can hang on to this for tonight?’

‘You can, sir, for now. Provided you come down to the station with me.’

A glimmer of hope appeared. Symongton returned to his wallet. ‘Good Lord. Here, officer, I’ve just found my licence after all. It’s in my wallet. It’s got my new address and all. Tell you what. You take down all the particulars from it while I go to a cash machine. Then, after an hour, say, I’ll turn up at the station to help you all I can. That leaves me free for a while to take this lady home and then I’ll report at the nick. No point in absconding, is there? Not with you having my car number and address.’

But the constable shook his head. ‘Sorry, sir. I’m not allowed to delay registering a charge like that.’

He cast a long look up and down the girl: the naked shoulders, the protrusive front and tight black skirt. His voice rang with a tinge of reassurance and perhaps regret. ‘I’m sure the cash machine’ll still be there, waiting for you, when you leave the station. And, no doubt, the young lady as well.’

Identity

Josh had barely reached the back corner of the bus station when he saw them coming. One, at most five feet tall but broad-shouldered and with a sag of belly that surmounted his holster-belt, must have come close to measuring equally in all three dimensions. A human cube. His colleague was tall and vacant-looking. Josh braced himself for yet another encounter with officialdom.

'Hey you, black fella. What you doin' hangin' around here?' 'I'm waiting for the midnight bus to Alabama.'

'Oh yeah? On your own and right here at the back o'the station?' 'I was keeping out of trouble.'

'Sure, sure.' With heavy irony. 'An' what you gonna do in Alabama?' 'I'm trying to trace an uncle of mine. It's my second summer of looking.' 'Takin' your time, ain't you?'

Josh fought down anger. It was always the same. At the airport, Immigration had detained him for over an hour.

'How do we know you aren't planning to stay in America?' they'd demanded. 'You don't but I'm not.' Josh thought: *I wouldn't stay here if you paid me. I hate your lousy, corrupt, racist country.*

'We don't want no tall stories, black man. We ain't jokin'.' 'I know.'

And now, as he crisscrossed the southern states by Greyhound, this was the fourth time they'd picked him up. The sus laws forbade loitering. Even in bus stations. Especially if you were black. Next thing, they'd want to check his wallet.

''Get in the car, big fella. We're givin' you a free lift.'

As the lamp-encrusted vehicle roared through deserted night streets, weariness invaded Josh. At Immigration he'd felt humiliated and contemptuous at the officers' automatic assumption that he wanted to stay permanently in this country. For once the perpetual conflict in him had eased: was he still at heart Jamaican, or, brought up in Birmingham and now at an English university, had he at last become a Brit? In an instant the greatcoat of history, from the slave trade to the penniless post-war arrivals on the Southampton quayside, fell from him. For now at least he was British. But how long would the feeling last?

The police station was brightly casual. A third officer lounged in a revolving chair, asleep at his desk. From a radio a night DJ gabbled maniacally. The Cube Man indicated chairs.

'Let's see your wallet, Mr Uncle-Seeker.'

He riffled through the contents with more-than-professional interest. 'Joshua Wallace. Plenty of cash here. How come?'

'I need it for travel. Even Greyhounds cost.' On impulse he added, 'The next one goes at 6.50.'

He wondered if he'd said too much. But Mr Cube paused, intelligence slowly surfacing. 'Hey, that accent. Where you from?'

'Birmingham.'

'Birmingham, Alabama, huh?' 'No. Birmingham, England.' 'Ah. Okay.'

The tone mingled disconcertment with wariness. And as always, it was working, the total, all-purpose defence – an English accent. Infallible. As it had been in Montgomery, Little Rock, Atlanta.

For a moment Cube sat silent. Then in a huge melting his face broke into curiosity.

'England. Is that a state of this country?'

'No. It's three thousand miles away. Across an ocean.'
'Gee.' The word carried wistfulness.

'What's it like, then – Birmingham, England?'

Josh's voice sank and trembled. 'It's great. England is just great.' Cube's head moved in slow nods, registering.

At last he gave in. 'Okay, fella. Let's have a coffee while you wait for your bus.'

Shame

From the moment of setting off, Sohail drove as if possessed.

'Sohail, take more care in the darkness. You will hit someone,' Rahat said. But it made no difference. Swerving to avoid other vehicles at eighty, careless of safety among the sudden- looming shapes and lunging headlights, he crouched rigid over the wheel. In the cold March air his face shone with sweat.

'Allah knows what must happen if it is true,' he muttered. Rahat tightened her arm round Nazli in the back seat. Tragedy came by other routes than accidents.

At the motorway exit the first seepage of dawn painted watercolours on a pale sky. At the University's shadowy gates Sohail drove up to the janitors' lodge and asked directions.

'I am looking for the Wilson Hall of Residence. For my daughter, Razeema.'

'You'll need to ask the Warden, Dr Wren. She'll show you.'

Leaving the car for the modern three-storey block was like disembarkation after the sea- sickness of a night-crossing. Sohail stood shivering while Rahat awoke Nazli from restless half- sleep and pulled a blanket round her. They hurried towards the door.

While they waited at the bell, *What will he do?* hammered in Rahat's brain. There'd been other cases, some uncovered, some still buried in sepulchral secrecy. The parents in Wolverhampton who'd strangled their daughter for the sake of honour, who'd been imprisoned for life. The family in Bradford who'd hidden their daughter's punishment till the strain became too great and they'd gone back home to Lahore to be safe from extradition. There was what you should do and what you dare do. Sickness invaded her like a plague. Why did

Sohail continually put his hand in his pocket. What had he hidden there?

'Hello.' The young warden wore a dressing gown and slippers. Her hair was tangled with sleep. 'Razeema? It's a bit early.'

'It is a most important matter.'

'All right, then. Come this way.'

At another time she would have enjoyed the new surroundings: the clean corridor with its neat pastel colouring, the doors bearing students' names and stuck-on paper images of Donald Duck, Tom and Jerry, The Terminator. Now, all she took in was her heart thumping, the clamp of breathlessness.

At a door with Razeema's name on it Dr Wren halted. Hesitation seemed to seize her. 'It's a bit early,' she said again. 'Wouldn't it be better if you came back later?'

'No. I wish to see her now.'

Dr Wren knocked. And it was as Rahat feared. Vomit rose in her gullet as a male voice answered, 'Come in.'

They filed in: Sohail, Dr Wren, then, halting in the doorway, Rahat and Nazli.

The room was tiny: a single bed, a small desk with chair, some pine bookshelves overhanging a sink. But what the eye met was none of these. In the bed, over the top of blankets disordered by over-occupation lay Razeema. And a boy. With a small cry Razeema shrank back under the covers, clutching a blanket to herself. But the boy still sat up, naked at least to the waist and angry.

'What the hell do you -?'

But Sohail's own anger overwhelmed him. 'What the hell? You may well ask. What the hell are you doing, as if it wasn't clear enough. I sent my daughter, my beloved daughter, here to become educated, not to associate with worthless layabout louts and lechers like you. But you don't care. You know no better. Polluting the most pure and beautiful thing in the world.

Destroying, for your own animal pleasures. Only a beast would do that. A pig or a snake! Well, I've seen enough. Get out! Get out! Are you deaf or mentally defective? I said, Get out!'

Under the fury of the tirade, the utter loss gaping at its heart, the youth sat stock -still, white-faced and mutinous. As Sohail's anger threatened to erupt into assault he shrank back, his hands flipped out from under the sheet. Sohail gripped the blanket and pulled but the youth countered with a tight grasp. Only when the outburst gave way to a silence like that of guns at an armistice did he with studied casualness get out of bed and, dragging a sheet to cover his nakedness, go over to a pile of clothes stacked on a chair and begin to dress. From time to time he looked back to Sohail, denying defeat. He sauntered out of the door.

Rahat's eyes turned to Razeema. This was where violence was most likely. Honour demanded it. She watched her husband's hand stray to the pocket where something – yes, she knew what it was, the guitar string - lay entangled or noosed. Yet the youth's departure seemed somehow to have made grief overcome anger. She loosened her grip on Sohail's sleeve as he turned to the warden.

'How could you? How could you do it? My daughter, who used to be such a lovely little girl, who I brought up to love and be worthy of love – you have turned her into a whore!' He drew a snatched sleeve across his eyes.

Razeema stared at him in terror. Unable to sustain his gaze, her eyes faltered and turned downward before she raised them again in defiance. 'You don't know Luke. You don't know how it is between us. You can't lay down how we must live.'

Sohail's rage brought him close to incoherence.

'How long has this been going on? How many other useless louts have you fouled yourself with?'

'He's not a useless lout and there haven't been others. Though the way you brought me up, shut off from boys, has made me go that way. We love each other. Don't you understand that? No, you don't because your own marriage was arranged, a financial deal, a sham. Literally, you don't know what you're talking about.'

But defiance had gone too far. This went beyond whoredom: it was disobedience. Sohail pressed his eyes shut to clear away moistness, then spoke with the cold voice of authority.

'Very well, you have chosen your path. You have not only chosen it, you have defended it. There is no going back. From now on you are not my daughter. You are an outsider, nothing to do with my family, nothing at all. I don't want to see you ever again, not to hear from you. And neither will your mother or your sister. You are a prostitute, a dirty cast-out worthless prostitute, and if you die in the gutter none of us will care. No, don't speak' – he silenced her with a shaking fist – 'I have heard enough of your shameful self-justifying.' He turned to Rahat and Nazli, lurking at the door in bitter tears. 'Come. We are going. Don't say goodbye. You will never see this – tart, this outcast again. We will not miss her. Come along.'

But in the corridor, with the door slammed behind them, grief came towering back. Going up to Nazli, he seized her in his arms and hugged her to him. For one minute, then two, he stood holding her with the love and passionate devotion of a father. At last his arms relaxed and he stood braced for bereavement, a world of loss.

'One good thing will come out of this.' Again he was addressing Dr Wren, his voice cold, drained of emotion. 'One good thing I have learnt. My younger daughter – I vow now and will keep my vow, that she will never, never, not on any account, go to any – *university!* '

As the three left down a silent corridor he stopped and, turning aside, gave Dr Wren one last accusatory, condemnatory glare. He neither noted nor understood the grief on the young warden's face, moved by another, different sense of loss.

Paying Her Way

Thelma kept looking up, glancing nervously over her shoulder as she scrolled down the website. But late at night in the deserted Computer Room, with the third years celebrating the end of Finals and the earlier years either in the Union bar or in bed asleep, she was safe enough. One by one, the ads under *Sugar Daddy* came up and were dismissed with gloom: too unctuous, too self-satisfied, too much of a show-off. Then Thelma paused, arrested.

Company director soon to retire, good company, cheerful, easy-going, seeks young attractive female, possibly student, for exclusive, perhaps live-in relationship, trips in UK and abroad. Allowance £1000 per month, discretion guaranteed.

A frisson of excitement made her catch breath. A thousand each month! It wouldn't just meet her living expenses. It would help to pay off her student debt, recently soaring past twenty-three grand. And he sounded a good sort. Yes. Yes. It had to be done.

And why not? Other girls did it. One night in the refectory she'd overheard Donna Wilson talking about the City stockbroker to whose out-of-town flat she travelled each weekend to earn her monthly £1300. The man in Thelma's ad was offering less than that but the chance of living- in might free her from the rent she paid for the hall of residence. And there could be savings elsewhere: on meals, drinks, entertainment.

Hands unsteady with excitement, she prodded the keys.

The *Receiving* tab came up almost at once. He must be at his computer right now. Within seconds a message appeared: confident and gentlemanly, even genial.

Thank you for replying. This sounds ideal! Let's meet for dinner one night and get to know each other. I suggest the Excalibur Hotel, Edgbaston some Friday night - say, at eight. Then there'll be no need for an early start the next day. How about the 14th? Godfrey.

Thelma consulted her diary. The page for the fourteenth trembled in her hand, as blank as fresh-laundered bedsheets.

*

There was no way of shaking off tension. The bus ride from the station and the walk from the stop to the hotel left her sweaty and breathless but for a penniless student there was no alternative. Maybe it would be her last journey on public transport for a long time. Company directors had cars: Audis, Bentleys, Porsches. At last the hotel came into view, tall and slim, pleasingly located in woodland set back from the road. This was a lifestyle beyond any she'd ever known. A surge of hope elated her, clamorous and demanding.

In the lobby she halted. Through plate-glass walls the interior of the restaurant was fully visible. Despite the start of the weekend it was almost empty – possibly reflecting the prices displayed on a menu at the door. In one corner a group of businessmen sporadically exploded over some risqué-sounding joke; three or four scattered couples barely disturbed the otherwise prevalent quietness; and in a far corner a man sat alone. Smart-suited, a good head of hair and decently built, he was handsome for his age. A friendly face. Better than she'd dared hope. He raised his head at sight of her and with summoned vigour she marched across.

'Thelma?'

She nodded. 'Godfrey.' They shook hands. He had a pleasant smile. 'Lovely to see you. Take a seat.'

Relief entered her, an inner whoop. This could be good. Yet tension remained. It annoyed her that she was not totally at ease. To sleep with an older man would be interesting. He'd probably be slower and gentler than the boys she'd had at Elmhurst Uni and in the neighbourhood around her home.

For some reason another thought also kept coming into her head: Angela A sort of anxiety, it must be, about how her mother might react. Need she really worry? Angela was independent- minded and fully aware of students' mores. She'd never jibbed in the past. Why should she now?

The question brought its own answer. Money. With this man, Godfrey, she'd be being paid for sex. Would that go beyond the limit of her mother's tolerance?

And yet why should it be? Money came into every relationship, marriage included.

Someone always paid. It was hypocrisy to deny it.

All the same, the word kept coming back: the P word. What if she chose the alternative – not telling, keeping the whole thing quiet? No, too risky. She imagined Angela hearing of the new arrangement from a friend, perhaps the mother of a fellow- student. Then, the word was bound to occur to her. She was Thelma's best friend and a good mother for all her brusque, matter-of-fact ways, but might she not use it, bring the word out in some moment of accusation or disgust? Secretly or openly, might she not think her daughter had become – a prostitute?

Godfrey disturbed her rumination. 'You said you were in your second year at Elmhurst. What are you studying? Tell me about yourself.'

Guardedly at first but gaining a certain security by imagining how, in the same situation, Angela would react, casually, brushing the question aside as if impatient at its unimportance, she gave a brief answer. In a moment or two, without showing haste, she took advantage after a moment's silence to shift the talk on to Godfrey's own work and life.

When he described office life and laughed at some of the odd characters in his firm she found herself joining in.

It was almost as if he was a neighbour at home, calling in to see Angela and have a chat, Thelma just happening to be there at the time.

*

'What's he like, then, your fellow?'

The whispered question brought on a jolt. 'What – what do you mean?'

'Come on, you know who I mean. Your *sugar daddy.*'

Had it come from Donna Wilson, who'd seen Thelma listening with interest to the cafeteria conversation about Donna's own sugar daddy, the question would have been less surprising; but this came from Leanne Halliwell. How had she found out? She couldn't have seen Thelma in the Computer Room or read the e-mail she'd written.

Where, then? Thelma's heart sank. If Leanne knew about Godfrey she must have got it from someone else. And so it was certain that everyone in the Uni would know. Oh God. And it was all a lie: the relationship hadn't even begun yet.

'*Sugar daddy?* What makes you think I've got one?'

'Someone saw you coming out of the Computer block after ten on Wednesday. You don't usually use the computers that late.'

'I do have friends, you know. I like to e-mail them now and then.' 'Oh yeah? Pull the other one, Thelma.'

Rebuffed and with a sceptical look of *Oh well, if you're going to be like that*, Leanne made her exit. Some minutes later, brewing herself a solitary cup of tea in an empty communal kitchen, Thelma wondered why she'd avoided answering. Because she disliked being the subject of gossip? Because it wasn't Leanne's business - or anyone else's? Or – the thought took minutes to surface – because the news might – would certainly – spread like wildfire. Until it came to the ears of – yes, that was it: Angela.

And all so unnecessary. People had such mass-produced, tabloid expectations.

Unlike the other men she'd known, mainly in their teens and twenties, Godfrey hadn't suggested sex that first night. At the station he'd said goodnight with a kiss that had been little more than formal. At their next meeting he'd shown her his house and the garden where he worked for most of his expanding leisure hours, the thing he most looked forward to in retirement: it clearly meant a lot to him. At third encounter they'd gone to the theatre and it had only been then, after late dinner at a high-class restaurant in the anonymous depths of Birmingham, that he'd steered her, without a word spoken, into his bedroom. As he'd joined her in the big bed with its starched, pure-white sheets, he'd seemed almost shy. It had been quite different from the bouts in student rooms, where doors had to be jammed shut with chairs under the handles, and at parties, where once or twice a door had been eased open, admitting a great wedge of din from the rest of the house, and someone had peered in. After that first night love-making became regular each weekend. At the month's end the never-mentioned payment into her bank account likewise became regular.

In every way, without being at all a father-daughter relationship, to Thelma their encounters seemed less like prostitution than any with the boys she'd had before. Yet maddeningly, against all reason, the feeling of restraint, the wish for secrecy persisted. *Why?*

Yet the mere fact of asking why was itself less than candid. She already knew the answer. The affair – was that what it was, or was it more like an old friendship? – would always feel covert, under-cover, while she failed to share it with the one person with whom she always shared everything. Everything came back to Angela.

*

'So you go round and stay at his place?' Standing at the sink, Angela attacked the washing- up with superogatory thoroughness.

'Just at weekends.'

The scrubbing of dinner plates continued with vigour. Angela moved to one side and increased by a smidgeon the radio's volume, only lowered a moment before.

'It'll help pay your way. The fees.'

'Exactly.' Thelma waited. Her mother thrust crockery into the drying rack.

Unusually, for an instant she hummed a snatch from some popular tune.

The front-door bell rang. When Angela hurried out to answer, a man's voice carried down the passageway.

'Good evening. I'm from *The Messenger*. I understand you have a daughter at university. I wondered if I could speak to her.'

'You've followed her here?'

'We're doing a feature on the ways students finance their studies. It's the fees, you know. Sometimes students use what you might call unorthodox ways…'

Thelma imagined her mother's face. The fury would be indescribable. Would she hit the man? It wasn't impossible.

'You can't talk to her – she has to go back to uni. Sorry to disappoint you.' 'Only one or two questions.'

'I told you, she's no time.'

But resistance seemed to encourage him. The coarse voice with its Estuary accent and habit of dropping every't' became more animated. At times he broke into laughter. He sounded the sort of man who was used to the aggression of pub brawls, more at home with a termagant than a caring mother.

'How do you feel about her seeing an older man at weekends, staying the night with him? A sugar daddy?'

There'd be a storm of outrage now – it seemed a certainty. But the explosion and all-too-probable stinging blow to the face never came. Angela's reply came with dignity, in a tone of contempt but without rage, only resignation.

'I'll tell you. You won't understand but I'll tell you. I'm proud of her. Have you got that for your sleaze-rag? Proud! Now I've answered your prying. Goodbye!'

As the door slammed, Angela, instead of returning to

the kitchen, could be heard climbing the stairs.

‘Don’t wait for me. I’ve some tidying to do.’

Tidying she’d never before mentioned. Doubts closed in on Thelma from all sides. Was her mother’s sudden disappearance genuine or merely a way of closing down discussion – a lie to smother her doubts? And the reporter - how did he brush off feelings of shame at his invasive, brazen questions? As for herself, who’d sworn a hundred times that she didn’t care what others thought or said, what were her own true feelings? In this hall of mirrors where reflections of reflections multiplied themselves down a gleaming gallery of deception - how could she know who was lying, why she should think deception might be necessary, and, most of all, for whom was the deception intended?

Python-A-Go-Go

It was dark in the sewer. Once Jake Truscott, kneeling on the tarmac in the hotel's yard, had shoved the manhole cover back into place above my head, daylight was blotted out. My sole source of light was the improvised potholer's lamp fastened round the hard hat he'd given me, run off a battery in the breast pocket of my overalls. If that gave out, I was sunk.

I cursed Truscott.

'I'm not a bloody sewer rat,' I'd told him. 'I came here as caretaker and odd-job man. You need a proper sewer-man for this.'

He stuck his jaw in my face. 'Listen, Bert Atkinson,' he said. 'The last man,

Ridsdale, did it, and so will you. It's not a foul sewer, only rainwater, and according to Ridsdale the brickwork's quite wide and high down there. You'll be able to stand up. Don't forget, with your reputation you're in no position to argue. Not after all the trouble you gave your last boss. Not after doing time for your petty thievery. You was lucky to get another job at all after that, what with your grudges and your mad ideas and practical joking. See? The manhole's in the yard, back of the hotel. Get to it.'

So I did. At the bottom of the fixed iron ladder I swung my head round to get an idea of things. The sewer's sides were old brick, weathered and crumbling, still there from when the old Victorian hotel was built, before they demolished it and put up the Excelsior. I couldn't stand up, whatever bloody Truscott said. I had to stumble along bent double, but at least there was no real smell, just a bit of a dank tang, a sour taste. And there wasn't much actual water, just wetness all round. I lurched along the four-foot-high circular tunnel till it joined another inlet and started to widen out and get higher. I could raise my head at last.

All the same, I had the jitters. I don't like darkness and I don't like being shut in. It's one of the things that gets me, like tyrannical bosses and people who do the dirty on me. I always feel kind of resentful, like as if I was wanting to get even with life.

Besides, there was water underfoot now, getting deeper, creeping up my waders to the knee, then the thigh. Every minute or two a drip of water from the roof would make a sharp slapping noise and I'd jump. Tense as a wire, I was.

What a bloody silly wild-goose chase, I thought. I was right, too. Some young starlet or maybe a glitzy old dame with more money than sense had dropped her diamond brooch down the washbasin. I'd had the waste-pipe off in her room to see if it'd lodged in the U-bend but it wasn't there. So Truscott announced it must have gone straight down to the sewer. It'd happened before, he said, the time he sent my predecessor, Ridsdale, down to find it. I doubt that. I doubt if he even expected me to believe it. You ask me, it was all PR to please the young sexpot or old turkey who'd lost it. But anyway, someone had to look for it and regular sewer-men don't do that sort of job, so it had to be me. Not surprisingly, I'd as good as decided, already, to have a quick glance round and then get back up, to the surface, the hell out of it all.

I pushed along a bit more, wading. Now and then yet another inlet let more water in. At one place the water was steaming, still half-hot from somebody's bath. I sniffed: bath-crystals. I can't tell you the delight: the sweet, warm, sort-of-elegant scent of bath-salts brings when you're down in the filth and cold. I flashed my head- light round one last time before turning to go back.

Then I glimpsed it. Oh God, the terror! At first I didn't twig, thought it was a submerged log or a flow of brown froth. But there was no mistaking the eye. An alligator's eye; and then another. Just lying there, looking at me.

Shaking, with my innards melting, I stepped back, slowly, desperate not to disturb it. One step, then another, then a third. I didn't breath. I couldn't take my eyes off it, like as if I was hypnotised. I kept on moving but with no real hope. He'd be hungry after being down here God knows how long. When they move, they move like lightning, alligators.

I knew what'd happened. People - the sort of rich nutters you get in Mayfair hotels, people who only value fashionable showing-off, not sense or reason - they buy baby alligators and keep them in the bath. Then, when the beasts start to grow, they go out at night and lever up a manhole cover and let them loose into the sewers. They haven't never a thought for those who work there. It happens, mate. It happens.

Never have I been so grateful. That lady having her morning bath had released hot water and that, I reckon, was why the ugly brute stayed put. Still walking backwards, I got to a bend in the sewer and in a step or two was out of the monster's sight. As the water got shallower, I turned and started to run, as quietly as I could. And ran and ran. When I got to the iron ladder and five feet up it, away from any snapping jaws, I kissed the putrid, slimy metal bars like they was a juicy bird I'd talked into bed with me.

I was that weak with shaking it took me minutes to lift the manhole cover.

When I'd surfaced I went for a drink. I needed it. While I was sitting collapsed in The Rosebery Arms the thought of the person that released that alligator to where it could have chewed me to a mince started burning inside me. Things like that do. They weren't getting away with it. I'd see to that. And it wasn't just a general decision to get even. 'Cause, the thing is, I knew who it was.

As a hotel handyman you get to know things. It's not that I'd seen the Yankee dame on floor fifteen of the Excelsior bringing home her new pet. And I certainly hadn't been in her room. Staff aren't allowed to do that, apart from the maids that make the beds. But I'd overheard her standing in the hotel foyer, chewing the fat with the guy in the next room, - while I was bringing cases down. She had that low, seductive accent that matched her reputation as the Delilah of the silver screen, with deep-blonde hair and a cleavage like the Cheddar Gorge. He was wearing a velvet jacket, waving his cigarette-holder about as if he was blowing bubbles.

'He's real cute,' I remember her saying. 'My sweet little ally-wally-gator. And growing so fast.' Yeah, I knew the one.

I thought hard, staring into my Worthington's. Then inspiration came. Glenys!

Yeh, Glenys was the answer.

No one at the Excelsior knows about Glenys. Often, you see, when I have to nip out of the hotel, I take a short cut through an alleyway near Shepherd's Market and across a quiet, cobblestone courtyard at the back of some high flats and offices.

There's not a lot in the courtyard, except for a club - the Python-A-Go-Go, it's called - a place I first noticed one hot summer lunchtime as I was passing. I stopped and looked. Standing in the club doorway was a girl, dressed in high heels. And nothing else.

Except a python. It was wrapped round her, bulging in and out where she did. I stared at it. Oh boy, I stared. Did I envy that beast.

I was late back to work that afternoon. I'd got talking to Glenys and she told me the snake was quite safe so long as it was fed regular – at the beginning of every third month. That was all it needed. Rest of the time it was harmless as a lamb. But if you just let it get hungry...oh mate! When it wasn't draped round her promontories and other points of interest she kept it in a cage. Safe as a kitten, she said; didn't even bother to lock the cage door. No one would disturb it till her act started, early evening. Now, sitting in the Rosebery Arms, it all came back to me, clear as a bell.

I had another Worthington's, two in fact. Then I got up. Outside it had started to rain but that didn't put me off. All the more chance that Mr Python - Monty, I called him -

would have been left on his own, alone. And he was. Through the alleyway, across the cobblestones and into the club entrance - not a soul. And there, in a side-room, bleak and silent, a cage. Better still - I couldn't believe my luck – next to the cage stood a big hamper obviously meant for carrying the python round in and, on the floor next to it, Monty himself. I wouldn't need the big holdall bag I'd brought. The only question was: what time of the month was it? I worked it out. The twentieth. I guffawed quietly. What luck! Monty had just eaten when I last saw him and so must be due a feed pretty soon now. He should have worked up just the right amount of appetite: not too much but not too little.

For now, though, he was sleepy. Steadily, as gently as I could without jarring his rippling, huge inner-tube of a body, I heaved his folds into the hamper. Heavy, he was. His eyes opened, his tongue flickered. I stopped. A minute later – it seemed like an hour - his lids closed again and slowly, in terror but heaving hard, I packed his body into the hamper. The lid slammed down and I drove in the wooden peg that fastened it. Straining every muscle, I lifted the hamper off the floor, then staggered out of the entrance. Glenys must be asleep or taking a day off, I didn't care. I panted into the courtyard's drizzling chill, unnoticed. I felt the most enormous upsurge of triumph.

*

'We can't let you in, Bert, without Truscott's permission.' Sandra at Reception was playing it by the book. 'You know what a row there'd be.'

'But Bert, I've told you: Truscott's out, fixing some conference that's due to come here. Meanwhile, the lady's plumbing needs doing.'

Sitting at her desk, the girl eyed my hamper. Through the dense basketwork you couldn't see the sleek tyres of flesh rolled up in it but my efforts at looking nonchalant when I'd lugged it into the lobby hadn't taken her in.

'What you got in there? I can't believe you need all that kit for a plumbing job.'

'Heavy pipe-joints, copper and lead. Honest, I -'

The tap of high heels cut me short. I began to look round, but the newcomer had already pushed forward to Reception. At once I recognised her.

'Oh, Miss Waldorf.' Sandra summoned synthetic delight. 'Can I introduce our handyman, Bert Atkinson, he does the repairs and maintenance around the hotel. He wondered if he could go into your room for a little while. It’s to do with the little problem about the plumbing.'

Miss Waldorf turned to me, hands thrown in the air with delight. I thought, this is the fancy-piece who’s pleasured half Hollywood, the whore who loosed the alligator that could have killed me. All the same, I had to admit she was glamorous, oh how glamorous, a work of art from the line of convex hips and the thrust of a tight bust all the way up to her eyelids, every inch slinky and svelte and well-manicured. Birds could have nested in her hair-do. She'd tugged open the front of her fur coat and it was as if it had burst apart with ripeness. Her eyes flitted up and down me. I felt like I was naked. Already.

'Why, sure, of course he can. Sure, I remember the plumbing problems but that's great by me. Come on up and in.' Her hand rested just for a moment on my shoulder, caressing-like, and a kind of sado-sexy thrill went through me like from an injection. 'Just follow me,' she said, laughing, palms held high in surrender. 'Just let me lead you on.'

It's what she did, too. In her room - all luxurious, it was, with silky dresses hanging in the open wardrobe and ritzy jewellery on the dressing table - she poured me a drink.

'You just sit down and make your-self feel real at home,' she said. 'Take as much of that gin as you like - well, not too much' - she laughed, flirtatious-like, under her eyelids - 'while I go and put on something a bit more casual, okay?' She grabbed a dress from the wardrobe and trotted into the bathroom. 'I'll only be five minutes.'

It was enough. Tiptoeing, I approached the hamper. It was heavy and unstable: Monty shifted his weight, restless. Hungry. I pushed open the bedroom door and dragged it in, towards the luxury double bed. I threw back the bedclothes. I unfastened Monty's lid.

I'd guessed it'd be hard, lifting him not just into the hamper this time but up to bed height, inert like he was, a dead weight. But when I tried, it seemed more than hard: impossible. I put my hands round his middle and tugged but he wouldn't move. I tried his tail. I could lift that but it didn't move the rest of him. There was nothing else for it. I had to lift him by the head and neck.

Glenys had told me pythons were non-venomous and lethargic but I couldn't have faced that hideous head if I hadn't wanted revenge on its silly, sexy bitch of an owner so much. I got the first stretch of the snake out and on to the sheet, then with a terrific heave the main trunk, then with less trouble the tail. Eight feet of him, thick as a water main. Panting like with asthma, I heaved the bedclothes back on the bed to cover him, and tidied the coverlet. You'll get a nice surprise tonight, Miss Waldorf, I thought. A real nice surprise. I chuckled as I zoomed back into the lounge.

I was just in time. I hadn't hardly sat down when the bathroom door opened and in she came. I gazed. A transformation. Short black cocktail dress coming halfway down her thighs. Four-inch spiky heels, The bird's-nest hair-do sort of released, flowing round her shoulders. And what shoulders! As for the rest of her...

She came up to me with her arms stretched out. Somewhere along the way she kicked her shoes off; she was smaller now. She dimpled at me from under her eyelashes like an innocent little girl confessing to having kissed a boy.

'I'm called Darothy,' she said, using an 'a' as usual 'And you're Bert. It's so nice we can be friends. I'm staying here on a six-month vacation to London, and I want you to know I just love your country, Great Britain.' She pronounced it very precise-like, as if it was a foreign word, to rhyme with rain. She stepped closer. 'Most of all,' she says, 'I think you Englishmen are just so cute.'

There was no mistaking her. I reached out and in seconds, without thinking, I had my hands round her, on her. Them forty-two inches. One hundred and six gorgeous centimetres. We didn't talk. We just moved towards the bedroom.

And as we was coming through the door the coverlet on the big double bed moved.

'No. No. Not there,' I said, jolting back a bit. The hair on the back of my neck was bristling with terror. 'Somewhere else.' In a sweat of relief I saw a way out, a lifeline for the drowning. 'Here,' I said, 'why not here? This lovely rose-patterned rug. It's really deep and soft. And inviting.'

She gave her laugh again; but she moved my way. 'Oh, you Englishmen,' she said, all coy and girlish. 'Do you know, I never realised how adventurous you are.'

I could have said the same for her. In thought, I transmit it to you now. The unveiling, like when the wraps slide off a statue of Venus, slipping down the marble till the final heart-stopping fall. The dizzying aroma all through the room, like as if a cloud of ether's covering you. The feeling I'm getting now, as we snuggle in the luxury of this three-inch-deep, woollen rug, a feeling like I'm a hamlet nestling at the foot of two mountains, a traveller lost in the Himalayas huddling into some warm, dark cave to save his life. The lightning-spasm at the height of a storm.

I didn't hear any soft thud or slithering. Dorothy's low moans and sudden outbursts of laughter must have muffled them. My head was too filled with images of smooth curves, of warm, rounded flesh, and the slow, dreamlike movements of adoration that were wrapping smooth, plump limbs round me. Even when Dorothy arched her back in abandon and I raised my body to bend forward and kiss points south, I thought the huge, bloated limb that reached out to embrace me - strangely, from behind - belonged to her, an arm or enveloping leg. It's only now that I recognise what they are, the coils binding us together, constricting our legs, our thighs, our whole bodies, tightening a little each time we breathe out.

I realise that, contrary to all we ever dreamed, ours is a union that will last. It'll last until the moment we die.

Heaven

'But what can it be like?' my aunt persisted. 'I mean, without your body or anything? Shall we be able to talk to each other?'

'Of course we shall. Not with our mouths, but we'll be able to, well, communicate.'

My mother didn't say how. She spoke awkwardly, with disapproval, feeling it was wrong to question what God had ordained for people after death. Yet for the twins in their eighties the question had become a matter of urgency. Except for that fact, the subject would never have surfaced in conversation.

Aunt Ethel pondered. 'It's as if we'll be like birds sitting on a telegraph wire.' 'It won't be like that, silly.

We'll be spirits.'

'That's how they make it sound.'

She meant the minister and other preachers at the local Methodist church. Both twins were Methodists but whereas Ethel worshipped at Queensborough, the grand classical building at the west end of the town, where a large and prosperous congregation could be relied on for fashion and gossip, Mother, to maintain her independence, attended a local chapel. 'We can't hope to understand it now. It'll be made clear at the time.'

Ethel pursed her lips and was silent.

Talk of religion was so rare in Mother's house, where I was staying on one of my regular visits to Shoreborough, that I was surprised when she raised the matter again later. It happened the following evening over bedtime cocoa after Ethel, who liked to watch more television than Mother, had returned to her bungalow next door, where she had moved after her husband's death to be near her sister.

'They have sealed warm baths, don't they?' Mother said suddenly in her slow, aged voice, apropos of nothing. 'I read about it. You get into a totally dark capsule where there's no sound or smell and you just float there. They say it calms you completely, as if time had stopped. Perhaps it's like that.'

It took me a moment to grasp what 'it' could be.

'Or a dreamless sleep?' I said when I caught on and after a pause to take in the new idea Mother said, 'Oh, I see,' and looked down again into her cocoa. She didn't seem shocked or disturbed by my secular view of death but neither did it affect her beliefs. 'I don't think there can be all that much talking,' she said in a while and I saw that, in prospect of eternity, she felt the old problem of Ethel's excessive loquacity troubling her still.

I visited more often after that. I still stayed at Mother's but more as housekeeper than as the guest I'd been until only a few years earlier. I did the shopping, obeying Mother's instructions to get fresh vegetables rather than the frozen ones Ethel favoured. I cleaned the kitchen floor and carpets, dusted the furniture and prepared the meals. Sometimes, for the sake of fairness, I went round and performed similar services for Ethel. Mother didn't approve, pointing out that Ethel had got herself a home help from the council without so much as enquiring whether her sister would like one. Mother was too lame with arthritis to go into town and her impaired hearing made it hard to telephone.

'I'll go down and get you a helper,' I offered, but she declined.

'They give you a form this long,' she said, creaking her arms out to a stretch of two feet. 'It would take me a week to fill in and Et would be bound to see it, wherever I hid it. You have to state your income.' Her face bore an old-fashioned look mingling disapproval with a certain self-respectful pride.

I tried to pacify her. 'You and Et were always very different,' I said.

'Mm.'

I could tell the words were well-chosen. Mother had

felt since childhood that she lived in her sister's shadow: Ethel, the go-ahead confident woman, full of initiative but also too inquisitive and bossy; Mary, shyer, more retiring but more sensitive to her own and other people's feelings. They had both, as illegitimate children whose mother had died at their birth, been fostered by the same lady in Shoreborough, a Mrs Conn, for the first two years of their lives; then gone to the same orphanage till they were sixteen; and thence moved to the local postmaster's house, where they lived in as domestic servants until Ethel had been allowed to learn typing and, liberated along with a whole generation of young women, gone out to work. Mother had always regarded that step as the beginning of the unfairness between them, the inequality of opportunity that led to Ethel's dominance in her life, the sister she needed and who was in so many ways a part of her, but from whom she struggled continually to separate herself, to escape the ever-present threat to her identity.

'She doesn't seem to realise,' Mother said. 'She thinks she has the right to know everything.' 'Everything?' I was slow on the uptake. Conditioned by the mass media, my mind conjured up imaginary scandals from the twins' early days: money, skulduggery, even sex.

'She opened my dividends one day,' Mother said, 'ones from some of the shares Joshua left me. Then she wanted to know how much I got in a full year. She's cheeky.' And indeed I remembered Ethel once saying with a great rolling of eyes and in the presence of a neighbour, 'She's worth thousands, you know. Just that one dividend was bigger than all mine put together.'

The talk moved on to old times: Mrs Conn, the orphanage, the postmaster's house. There'd been Mum's engagement to Raymond, a rough lad who loaded delivery vans at Yaxley's Department Store and was killed in a motor bike accident; and some years after that the twins' marriages in the same year, 1930, to two Shoreborough men, Joshua and Harry. We talked of Mother's unhappiness with the moody and at times violent Joshua, and of the divide between the twins in 1939 when Ethel and Harry, at the outbreak of war, both joined the Air Force. About this, the two sisters and Harry had often reminisced, and now Mother repeated some of the old stories. But whenever I turned the conversation even faintly in the direction of religion, Mother jibbed. 'I don't want to talk about it.'

All the same, there was one visit, close to the end, when she did talk. She had suffered quite a severe stroke the previous summer and after rushing down to Shoreborough Hospital to see her I visited the town regularly, to be as close at hand as possible. Ethel, though herself unwell, visited by taxi whenever her health permitted.

'Bring my dress from home, will you?' Mother asked as the bell rang and I rose to go. 'The new, grey one. Bring it in next time you come.'

'But will you be getting up so soon?' I said. 'Will you need it before you go home?' 'I sometimes get up, here. They wheel me into the sun lounge.'

'Do you need your new dress for that?' 'Mm.'

The sound seemed meant to convey yes, and at the next weekend I took the dress in, along with the shoes and other clothes she'd asked for. None of them seemed especially smart - with Mother the term 'new' was by then only relative - and perhaps this was why it was only as I took them out of their holdall bag that the true reason why she wanted all these Sunday-best clothes dawned upon me.

'Are you getting up more often now?' I asked, absurdly feigning ignorance; but she didn't answer. It was enough that those she met would see her at her best - Mrs Conn, Joshua perhaps, Raymond.

'How's Et?' she asked. 'She never tells me.'

'Not very well. The doctor told her to rest. A nurse comes in at night.' 'I mean, her clothes.'

'Clothes? All right, I think. She dresses well.'

The news seemed to calm her. 'It's nice to be well - dressed, meeting people.'

'I summoned up the question I'd wanted to ask ever since the twins' earlier conversation about heaven. 'Mum, do you - do you want very much to meet Joshua again?'

The jaw stiffened, the old-fashioned look flitted to her face again. 'We'll all be different there. We'll be spirits. There'll be others...' 'Raymond?'

'Mm.' This time there was no mistaking the pride, the distant grey look of loss. This was something big in her life, a sustaining warmth at the far end of it.

'He used to stand up to Et. You know?' A faint mischievous smile flickered about her lips. 'It used to make me feel confident. Free.'

'And Joshua didn't? Didn't make you feel like that?' 'No. Never.'

Yet it wasn't wholly true. Joshua had 'stood up' to Ethel, had indeed had rows with her to curb her meddling in his and Mother's affairs. Perhaps it was just that his anger didn't bring confidence while the parcel-loader's cheeky cockiness did.

'Tell Et to look after herself,' Mother said as I left on what turned out to be my penultimate visit: before the final one, the midnight call that brought me back to hold her hand through the night, hoping she recognised me, hoping the stroke that tied her mouth hadn't cast a frost over her mind, hoping she knew she was never for one second alone as she moved into another, strange and frightening world.

The crossing-over came with the first crack of dawn. And though in the end unfathomable, those final words stayed with me ever after. Words about and for Ethel, not Raymond, they made me feel Ethel had won, outstaying the one man who, had he lived, might have freed Mother from her twin's lifelong dominance. As things were, all that remained for Mother was to make sure that she and Ethel met their Maker, and their loved ones, wearing their Sunday best.

The Eye of Truth

'It's all very well, Ron. But who’s going to pay the mortgage, the way you spend?' Ron settled on the arm of her chair. His voice went soft. Seductive, like it always did. 'Listen, Dora, there's no problem about money, I've told you that. We've got your pay, and the rent from the cottage your dad left you. As for me, you've seen my Porsche, spotless inside and out from bonnet to boot. You've been out in it lots of times. A man without means couldn't afford that. Then there's my pad. Look, I'll show you again.'

He reached in the breast pocket of his suit - she had to hand it to him, he did wear a suit, the only man she knew who did - and drew out the wad of photos.

'Here. Just look.'

She gazed at the now-familiar image. Huge and gable-fronted with black Tudor-style beams, the house was her heaven.

'See, that's the double garage. Porsche goes in there, and there's still room for the other one. And the grounds, front and back. You should just see them.'

The idea lodged. 'Ron, couldn't we - couldn't we go to London one weekend and stay in this place? I mean, it seems such a shame, living here in this pokey ex-council house when we could be relaxing- like, really living. It's only just down the motorway. I don't mean regularly, only now and then. Couldn't we?'

Doubt shrouded him like a cobweb. 'It's the work, Dora. Keep me at it all hours, they do, weekends and all. Even off duty, I'm still on call. It's a twenty-four-hour, seven-day job, the insurance industry.'

'What do you insure, Ron? You never tell me.'

'Pretty well anything. Confidential, of course. I can't talk about it to anyone. My, oh my, no. That'd be a breach of professional whatsits. Ethics.'

She joined in his chuckle, but more mirthfully. 'You are funny, Ron, talking like that. You make me laugh.'

He leaned over her, put his arm round her shoulder. 'Well, there you are, my darling. Take me or leave me. But if you'll have me, I'll always be true to you. Sure as I stand here. For ever.'

'You're not standing, Ron. You're sitting.'

'You know what I mean. My heart is true. Remember all the flowers I've bought you. They didn't come cheap. And how I've been willing to live with you here, in this shanty. I know: it's all a shop assistant can afford. Not that I don't like it,' he added in haste. 'I love it because you're in it, light of my life.'

'I do love you, Ron. Ever since you chatted me up in that club, the first evening. And when I've asked you back here. You talk such rubbish, you set me all giggling.'

'You're not casting nasturtiums on my whatsits? Credentials?'

'No, love, course not. You've got a good sense of humour: GSOH, they call it in the ads - I've often looked at those. And you're friendly and generous. A real good sort. It's just - well, the practical side.'

'No problem there. Just you think about it, Dora. Don't think too long, though. Snap me up quick, while supplies last. Unrepeatable offer. Hold on.'

He leaped to the bleep of the mobile phone in his pocket and, holding it tight to his ear, walked from the room into the kitchen.

'An urgent meeting,' he announced when he came back. 'Oil tanker, ten million tons. I'll have to go. Back soon, I hope.'

'A meeting, Ron? At this hour? Can't be.'

'You just don't know. No peace for the wicked, there ain't - only a joke. 'Bye, then, my love, till we meet again. Time for a kiss. Think over what I was saying.'

When the door shut, through a slit in the curtains she watched the huge blue car slide away from the house. Then, crossing the room, she flipped through the pages of the directory.

'Private Investigations Limited?' she said. 'I want you to do a job for me.'

The man's voice was as restrained as his knock on the door. He wore a suede jacket over the brown, button-down shirt and slim- line trousers. 'I won't take tea, thanks.' He seemed polite and well-spoken.

'Have you made any progress, then?' Dora asked.

'Well, yes we have.' The man raised his eyes to her. 'May I ask, first, Mrs -?' 'Miss.'

'Miss Weelsdon. How close is your emotional attachment to the gentleman we're concerned with: Mr Gardner?'

With faint embarrassment she raised a hand, indicating the sweater on the back of a chair, the slippers Ron had left, as usual, under the sewing table. 'I live with him,' she said.

*

'Mm. Then I'm afraid what I'm going to say may come as a shock. I hope you'll be prepared for it.'

Dora remained silent.

'The fact is, to begin with the work side of things, Mr Gardner isn't at all what he told you he was, not an insurance manager. In actual fact he's a chauffeur. It's a job that explains - quite a lot.'

'Yes. I think I see. The car, you mean? And the mobile phone, the calls at all hours.' 'Quite.'

'But there was the big house in London. He had snaps of it.' 'He had indeed. Like this one.'

The young man held out a photograph, his hand covering the top edge. In a moment he removed the hand. *Staverton Whitehouse*, the overprint read. *Registered estate agents and property dealers*. His face soft with concern, he waited.

'I did wonder,' Dora said at last. 'But I couldn't know for sure.'

'It would be why he always paid cash when he took you out. No respectable company would give him credit.'

'I suppose not.' 'May I go on?'

'There's more, is there?' For the first time, she seemed agitated. 'I'm afraid so.'

'Other - women?'

'Yes. Before you, three. One he married but she divorced him. Then two he lived with, serially, sponging on their money, getting free meals and accommodation. When the perks ran out, he left. He doesn't sound a good prospect as a husband, Miss Weelsdon. I have to say that in all honesty.'

A sort of animation revived in Dora's white face.

'He's got a job. He earns good, steady money - I saw his bank statement.' 'But it won't support his lifestyle. Hence the deception.'

'Did he cheat on these women? Did he two-time them?'

'Not that, exactly. But he won their favours with lies and lived off their savings.' 'I suppose so. Because they let him.'

There was a silence. The young man placed his report on the sofa and made as if to leave. 'I'm sorry to have to say all this. I only hope you'll agree that PI has done its job thoroughly.'

She nodded, a faint forlornness lingering.

The action moved him to pity. Halting at the door, he made a last offer. 'Would you like me to meet this man, Miss Weelsdon? Perhaps get him to call one day when you're out and confront him with his deceptions? Try to shame him into decency? We could have bouncers at hand, in case of trouble.'

This time, she shook her head. 'Don't tell him anything,' she said. 'You've done your job. I'll pay you.'

'Of course, you'll refuse his proposal?'

She got up and moved to the door. When she spoke, a rime of defiance stiffened her voice. 'I shan't. I shall accept.'

The young man froze, incredulous. 'Even though he's a

trickster? Even though he'll leave you as soon as you're broke?'

'I don't care. I've had enough of being alone. He sticks with his job; he's steady with a woman while the money lasts. *While she makes it last.*' Her face broke into a smile. 'He gets me laughing. 'He says like poetry things. I'll manage, you'll see.'

At the garden gate the private eye paused and looked back. A tremor of surprise raised his eyebrows. How happy she looked, watching him go. Waving, she gave a small skip. 'Insurance manager,' she called out, laughing. 'With a peaked hat in his car boot! He'll need real discipline in his home-life. And I'll have to play the lady, married to one of those!'

At First Sight

‘If this is going on any longer,’ Ed grunted, ‘I’d better have some refreshment.’ Vi loved the masculine way he lunged forward to press the bell-push sitting like a huge verruca on his desk.

‘A cup of coffee, please,’ he said when Travis appeared. ‘Hadn’t it better be two?’ Travis moved her eyes towards Vi. ‘Oh yes. I suppose so. Two, then.’

Vi giggled. The action made the shiny golden spirals of her hair shake l ike brass shavings. She looked at Ed, bright-eyed. ‘Shall we finish the inventory?’

With the sigh of a deflating balloon Ed returned to his documents. ‘Two towel racks.’ He might have been intoning a roll call. ‘Curtains. Staircarpet. Toilet-roll holder.’

He leaned forward as if studying his desk. It was sweet, the way his jowl doubled in size when he lowered his head. There was a silence.

‘Is that the end, then?’

‘Mm?’ A lovely, deep, grumpy voice. But slurred, abstracted. As if her question had woken him from groggy sleep.

‘I mean, is it the last – the toilet-roll holder?’

He didn’t directly answer, instead speaking into the space behind her left ear, making it tingle, so that she raised a heavily ringed hand to rub it.

‘Toilet-roll holders! Ugh! I spent five years training for this job and what have I done for twenty-three years? Listed toilet-roll holders! TWENTY THREE YEARS! Murderers get less.’

‘Poor you.’ Vi felt sympathy surge. Such a handsome, well-dressed man. Concessively, she added, ‘Though they are necessary.’ ‘Mm?’

‘I mean, we do have to have them.’

‘Have what?’ ‘Toilet-roll holders.’ ‘Yuck!’

‘Unless you keep them on the floor.’ ‘The holders?’

‘No, the rolls.’

There was a silence. Vi felt she should speak. ‘It’s very good of you, helping with my move like this. I needed a smaller house, you see. Downsizing. After Ray died.’

It didn’t seem to work. The conversation had no zip. In fact, there was no conversation. She hurried on.

‘It was awful, the way he went. He was in the garage re-charging the car battery when he took hold of a live wire – and the shock killed him.’

She waited for a response but the lawyer seemed absorbed in studying her face.

‘He was a lucky man, Ray,’ he said at last. ‘Such a loving wife.’

‘Not that it’s much comfort now, of course.’ Vi found his gaze disconcerting, even despite its kindness. ‘Ray was a lovely man. It was so sad.’ She put on a tragic, winning smile.

‘You were lucky. My wife left me for another man.’ ‘Oh, how terrible!’

‘It was after separate income taxation came in. You get two allowances now instead of just one, So I gave her half my savings. Next thing, she’d gone.’

‘Oh! I knew as soon as I saw you. I said to myself, “That’s a man who’s suffered greatly.”’

‘I only saw her once more.’

‘When you went to appeal to her better nature?’

Ed shook his head. It made his jowl quiver again, excitingly. ‘No. She hasn’t got one.’ ‘To give her a piece of your mind, then? And quite right, too.’

‘No. It was when she came to demand her half of the jointly-owned house.’

Vi stood up, outraged. Then sat down again. ‘Well, I never.’

For a minute only the wall-clock’s tick was audible. The thought of this lovely man losing half his house – the process of dividing it was hard to imagine but Vi was sure there must be some way – brought a prickling to the back of her eyes. Not unlike the prickling when she'd put on too much mascara, except that was at the front.

With alarm she remembered her schedule. Oh dear, she'd be late for her date with that exciting Hungarian she'd met at the bridge club and persuaded to ask her to lunch.

'Shall we – I mean, do you think we should - get on with..?' She indicated Ed's conveyancing papers. She didn't like to be too brutally precise.

'Get on?'

'I'm thinking of the time. You're a busy man.' 'They went to the Bahamas, you know.'

'Really? I didn't know that.' A pause. 'Who exactly?'

'She didn't need my money at all. He was as rich as Croesus.'

'Oh, what a moneygrubber! I've heard of people like that. I just wonder how they do it. I know I –'

'But for her, I could have retired early. By now I'd be lying in the sun with a sunshade and a Bacardi.'

Through the window Vi surveyed the steady downpour. 'Oh, I hope you'd have more company than that. What you need is a lovely lady who'll –'

But at the mention of ladies Ed snorted - like a walrus, Vi thought. From regret at what he'd missed, no doubt. She changed the subject.

'Ray was a great one for sunbathing. He used to get brown as a berry. Except on the bits he didn't expose, of course. It was his best point, his tan. He had that sort of skin, dark and *meaningful* – know what I mean?'

'Croesus had his own yacht out there.'

'People sometimes thought he was Italian, Ray. He looked the type. Romantic.' 'Their honeymoon went on for three months. He was off work *three months*.' 'I'm not saying you're not romantic as well. Comparisons are odiferous, I always think. He hadn't your lovely gruffness. And his ties were in such *awful* taste.'

'She'd like that, a three-month holiday. All without so much as touching the seventy grand she stole from me.'

‘Oh! *Grand*, now. Don’t tell me. I heard it on television. It’s a thousand, isn’t it?

‘Grand’ makes it sound really swish and exciting, makes you think of Lamborghinis and Porsches. You have charm, you know, just like Ray. No, not like Ray.’

Again, the deep, piercing look. ‘You’re very companionable. You say such nice things.

‘I mean them.’

He looked down again. ‘They don’t work, you know, the rich. Not once they’ve made their first million. They employ managers.’

‘I’m always glad Ray left everything to me. That live wire might have robbed me of a husband but at least I’m well cared for.’

The wall-clock’s tick seemed suddenly loud. Vi looked at her watch. Ten past one. She’d missed her lunch date. Missed meeting that luscious Hungarian – what was his name? Laszlo, was it? No, that was that other one, last year. She’d have to apologise when they met again. Tell him she’d been suddenly taken ill with a temporary but violent distemper – she liked that word: *distemper* - and then found the telephone didn’t work. She’d have to be *maximo charmissimo* about it.

She gripped the handbag on her lap like a handlebar. ‘Does that finish our – business, then?’ She smiled to soften the efficiency of the question.

Ed grunted. ‘Suppose so. I need some lunch. Make me fat but what the hell? You have to eat.’

‘Of *course* you do. Of *course.*’ An idea came from nowhere. ‘I know, why don’t we go down the road and eat together at that little Greek restaurant? They have moussaka and paklava and –‘

Had the walrus act come back? No, he was getting up from his chair, levering himself like a dugong she’d once seen on television. Oh dear, she mustn’t mix her metaphors. Miss Shrimple at school had hated that.

Ed took his coat from a peg and wrestled his arms into the sleeves. He was overweight but that wouldn’t matter if he took things gently.

'The money your husband left..?' he began and Vi was only too pleased to tell him more. They moved to the door.

'You're right about me needing to retire,' he said and Vi felt a kick of joy that he'd taken in something she'd said. It was nice, a gruff, silent, strong man doing that now and then. Not that it really mattered.

'Yes, I am. Honestly, you should. Now that you're financially secure.' They emerged into a steady deluge.

'Here, come this way with me.' Vi put up her Japanese-style umbrella and took Ed's arm. It was lovely, having a soul-mate, a kindred spirit. And people didn't often really click like this, two hearts beating as one. She gave his arm a tiny hug. And when, a little later, he suddenly slowed down and asked, 'Ray's legacy – was it unencumbered?' it brought her pleasure to reassure him that it was. The question might sound rather bald and mercenary but it didn't mean money was Ed's main interest. A solicitor would be interested in a technical, legal detail like that. It didn't mean he didn't love her or feel the warmth and companionship she'd seen in his face. He might *partly* care about her money but that was understandable: you had to be realistic. His financial questions were only part of his funny, crusty manner, things he asked because he wanted to have everything clear and business-like.

'A straightforward bequest,' she repeated when he answered, snuggling up a bit more, licking raindrops from her upper lip. 'Really generous. More than enough for two.'

Hetty

I'd had a night out with the girls the previous evening, Friday, so they wouldn't expect to see me again. At six, after Dad would have finished watching *Final Score*, I rang home for a leisurely chat. After that, a goodnight call to the children, who'd gone for their fortnightly weekend with Edwin. Then it was into jeans and a T-shirt, a quick smuggle of my suitcase through the side door to the car in the lean-to garage, and I was away.

The sheer enormity of it was half the thrill. The sense of a hidden life. As I edged through the traffic on the High Street Mr Philpott from the golf club spotted me and waved; and I waved back. Earlier in the month I'd dropped his wife a note in which I'd casually mentioned a weekend away with my walking group, so there was no chance of discovery there. The excitement of secrecy! I was a bank robber getting away with it. Again and again.

I'd met Robin three years earlier when I sifted his number out from the myriad websites offering what he supplied. God, I was nervous that night. It seems hilarious now, but I was broiled in sweat as I drove through outer Birmingham's sprawl and slid into the car park under the Westchester Hotel. As I reached the room I'd booked and changed into my new black cocktail dress and court shoes I got the trembles and had to sit down until my heart stabilised a bit. Twice I dropped my lipstick before applying it successfully. The room was high on scent. All I'd signed on for by e-mail was a two-hour dinner with my unknown escort. Robin didn't even know I'd booked the room on Floor Four. It was a fall-back, a precaution. All the same, sex pervaded my every action and thought, mind and body alike.

He was tall, dark and strikingly handsome – far handsomer than anyone who'd look twice at me for a non-paying relationship; the adipose folds of middle age had seen to that. Worst of all, the beetroot crumpet-mark on my left cheek where scalding water had jetted out from a pressure cooker in my schooldays turned men off like a stopcock. Hadn't it been one of the things that cleft me from Edwin? He always denied it but I wasn't born yesterday. With men appearances rule.

We exchanged the usual patter. Names (but I gave him a false surname and he asked for no address), marital status (both divorced), number of children (both three). We had things in common. I'd done it all before at *The Sphinx* behind Digbeth, where I'd sometimes gone looking for sex, but after one or two club visits the effort of constantly beginning all over again, the uncertainty of never knowing what was in store, made me ditch one-night stands. I needed to know what would happen and I needed it to happen without hassle, when and as often as I wanted. With no worries afterwards. That way I could concentrate on my job, my children, my life. Sure, I pay. But we all pay, one way or other.

My chief worry was that I wouldn't find him attractive. I was risking the awful clash of bodily need and revulsion. But I needn't have worried. At thirty-six, with the slim build and fitness of an athlete, he was gorgeous. Robin. Immaculately dressed, charming, the man who had everything including a hint of that faintly detached, aloof mystery that makes a man irresistible, he seemed genuinely interested in me. A touch of Canadian accent, I thought, and sure enough, he was born in Toronto. A breath of the wider world. At the end of two hours of talk, almost but not quite tender, we both knew the next move. I took his arm as we walked from the restaurant to the lift. It was the most natural action in the world.

In a moment, when Robin left me alone in the bedroom, I checked my mobile for messages, as I always do now. The coolness of it! They say doctors who murder their patients have that thrill: the euphoria of a huge confidence trick. It's the only parallel I can think of.

And so our third anniversary came round. Over three

summers and winters, in hotels and country cottages up and down England the sex had grown better and better. We'd taken it in turns to book places to eat, Robin always ordering candles and soft music, the best wine. Never less than attentive, gentle and humorous but always respecting the privacy of my other, real life. Seeming never to see my wounded cheek, wonderfully sensitive. And no one knew a thing.

From the start there'd been questions I longed to ask. Where did he live?

What was his other job, his day job, if he had one? How long could a career such as his – the term *service-provider* kept coming to mind – how long could it last? Was he saving for early retirement? How many other visits did he pay? There must have been others: it was unthinkable for a man like that not to be in demand, fees and all.

I'd felt a physical jolt when they came up on line: £200 for one hour, £280 for two,

£500 for a night. But never was money better spent - Edwin's alimony and the surplus left, after household expenses, from my salary at Bestingham's. If he'd opened an account with us I could have given testimonials. Oh, I could have done that.

But I had my secret, too. The doctor's warning wasn't in any measure what had driven me to the internet and so to Robin; I'd done that because I wanted control of my body and my life without the need to support a man. But now a visit to Dr Coulson had reinforced my determination, my commitment to pleasure.

'It's no easy to forecast the course of the illness,' he'd said in that gentle Scottish accent of his. 'Diabetes of your kind, Type Two, can be contained for many years if you're careful and take the tablets.'

'And if I don't? If I forget?'

That soulful Highland face. 'I wouldna say you seem the sort who'd forgeit.' 'But if I did?'

'It could put you into a coma. At the least.' 'I see. I

won't forget.'

'I'm sure you won't. But oh, jest one more wee thing.' He lowered his glance. 'Controlling your weight can help.'

I thanked him and took the prescription. Like him, I trusted myself. Now I had something to live for, not just my job and my children but Robin, too. I wouldn't make mistakes.

And yet I did.

It was like one of those stories where someone devises the perfect murder – until he makes one fatal slip. Well before it was time to set off, I'd already packed my suitcase. My jeans and t-shirt lay ready on the bed upstairs. I'd put down the phone after ringing Dad and the children. Then the doorbell rang. It was Mrs Philpott, come about the club's competition next week. I put on my beaming smile – how I enjoyed acting the part – and invited her in. We talked in a leisurely way and when the talk threatened to dry up I found myself adding to it, piling on the deception of having time to spare. It was forty minutes past my usual time when I finally got away.

But Robin was waiting unfussed, as patient as he was understanding and attentive.

We had a lovely dinner among the roses and the scented candles and the shining damask tablecloth and napkins. We talked more intimately than usual. He spoke for the first time of his work as an investment manager – he was clever as well as handsome – and of his hopes and aspirations. I told him Edwin was all over now, a ghost from the past. The future offered new adventures.

As we walked from the hotel's restaurant past the smiles and bows of the waiters I snuggled up to him, enchanted by the script that never grew stale, as if it would go on for ever. It was only in our suite, while he was in the bathroom and after I'd checked for messages, that I reached into my bag among the little bottles and the powder puff and the wad of bank notes, looking for Dr Coulson's pills (no, not the life-preventing ones but those that *sustained* my life) and my fingers grasped – nothing.

Like a fast-track film my mind raced. I must have left them in the bathroom as I sleepwalked through the afternoon preparations. With me it isn't at times of haste that I forget things; it's when I have time in abundance. Even then I might have remembered but for Mrs Philpott's appearance. I cursed the woman.

How long had I been without them? Since that morning. But no, damn, damn,

Edwin had called early for the children, interrupting the usual breakfast routine, and I hadn't taken them then, either. By the time I got home again I would have been thirty six hours without medication. I could fall into a coma. Or, according to the Family Health Guide, worse. Much worse. I was in terror.

At last – how long would the bloody man take getting ready? – Robin came back. He was smiling maddeningly, not a care in the world.

'Robin,' I said, 'there's something I have to tell you.'

'Hey, gently, darling.' Still smiling. 'You've had a long drive. Take it easy. We've got the whole night.' He put his arm round my waist, easing me towards the bed.

'No, don't. It's something vital. Urgent.'

'Come *on* now. There's only one urgency for us, tonight.'

Normally I might have explained. But tonight - a mere thirty minutes ago – there'd been something new and close between us. Our talk at dinner had taken us, I realised too late, to the brink of love. A concealment confessed to, any kind of deception, could destroy that. And I was angry, with us both. For minutes I protested, ranting down his caresses and wheedling. It was as if *he*, damned man, was the one wanting pleasure. God, who was paying for this?

'I have to go,' I said. I reached in my bag for the money. 'Here, you can have the whole amount if you want it. I've taken up your time.'

He stood there with his head tilted, a pose he'd never adopted before. That touch of aloofness I so loved had changed. To wryness? Or cynicism? I didn't have time to decide.

Did adrenaline or exhaustion interact with diabetes, did it accelerate the effects of lacking insulin? My head swam. I sat down on the bed here in this room, tortured. He didn't make any attempt to support me, just took the money. As I lay – on this coverlet - struggling for breath, he took a mobile from his coat pocket and phoned. *Yes dear, as it happens I am free tonight. Mm, twenty miles? I could be round in half an hour. That okay? Lovely. See you, then.*

All in the same understanding voice he'd used with me.

'Shall I get you a taxi?' he said as he put on his coat. But I was taking no favours from him. The door clicked shut.

I, too, have my mobile. And, at home, my ansaphone's ready, taking down the words I'm now thinking, even speaking out loud. The dizziness grows worse and thoughts of my children swim in my head. But what use would it be to ring Edwin? What could I say? How could I face him? And the children would find out. Everything. More to the point, no one could get here in the short time the Health Guide allows between coma and final stillness.

Meanwhile he's escaped unscathed. I've no real name for him, no address, no identification for the man who left, cool as a murderer. He's making off from the vilest deed of all, the betrayal of love, the perfect, undetectable crime.

www.ingramcontent.com/pod-product-compliance
Ingram Content Group UK Ltd.
Pitfield, Milton Keynes, MK11 3LW, UK
UKHW042000190726
13854UKWH00005B/2077

9 781789 552393